Children's Books:

Kevin and his Magic Turtle

Sally Huss

ISBN: 0692381503
ISBN 13: 9780692381502

Kevin sat on a bench at the edge of the sea and watched the boys and their turtles play in the water. They splashed and they dove and as they surfaced, the boys screamed with delight.

When they returned to the shore they told of the wondrous things they had seen in the magical world below.

The next day came. Kevin raced to the seashore and gave proof of his birthday to the official in charge. The official stamped the paper and said, “Give this to the Turtle Keeper,” then pointed to a shed where another man stood next to a stack of turtles.

“Happy Birthday,” said the official, as Kevin dashed off toward the shed.

The Turtle Keeper took the paper and gave Kevin the finest turtle in the stack. “Now remember,” said the Turtle Keeper, “feed your turtle well. Give him lots of fresh air and plenty of sleep.”

“I will. I will,” promised Kevin, as he struggled toward the water with the massive turtle under his arm.

He plopped the turtle in the water and jumped on its back. Now he too would know the secrets beneath the sea.

Kevin and his turtle swam out to where the other boys were playing in the water.

“Dive! Dive!” commanded Kevin. But the turtle was reluctant. They were just beginning their life together and he wanted to begin slowly. Not Kevin. “Dive! Dive!” he commanded again.

The turtle did as he was ordered to do and down they went.

Under the water, other boys and their turtles were exploring the water wonderland. Some were diving to great depths. Others were playing games with creatures they had found.

Kevin joined a group of boys who were playing water hockey with mallets made from coral sticks. They would bat a mollusk shell around and knock it into nets of sea fern.

Back and forth they swam. Up and down they dove. Of course, occasionally they would have to come all the way up to the surface for air. Kevin stayed the longest and played the hardest. By the end of the day his turtle was exhausted.

Kevin, on the other hand, was filled with energy and excitement over his day's adventure.

That evening Kevin left his turtle on the shore and ran home before dark, only to return the next morning at daybreak.

He had to awaken his turtle. “Let’s go,” said Kevin. “The day is beginning and there is so much to see and do.”

Onto his turtle's back he climbed and out to sea they swam.

"Dive! Dive!" demanded Kevin.

The turtle did as he was told.

They passed a herd of seahorses and a garden full of sea anemones.

Then they came upon a galaxy of starfish.

"Deeper," pointed Kevin. So deeper they dove, down to where the big fish swam.

There were yellowtail tuna, marlin with swords, and swordfish with spears…

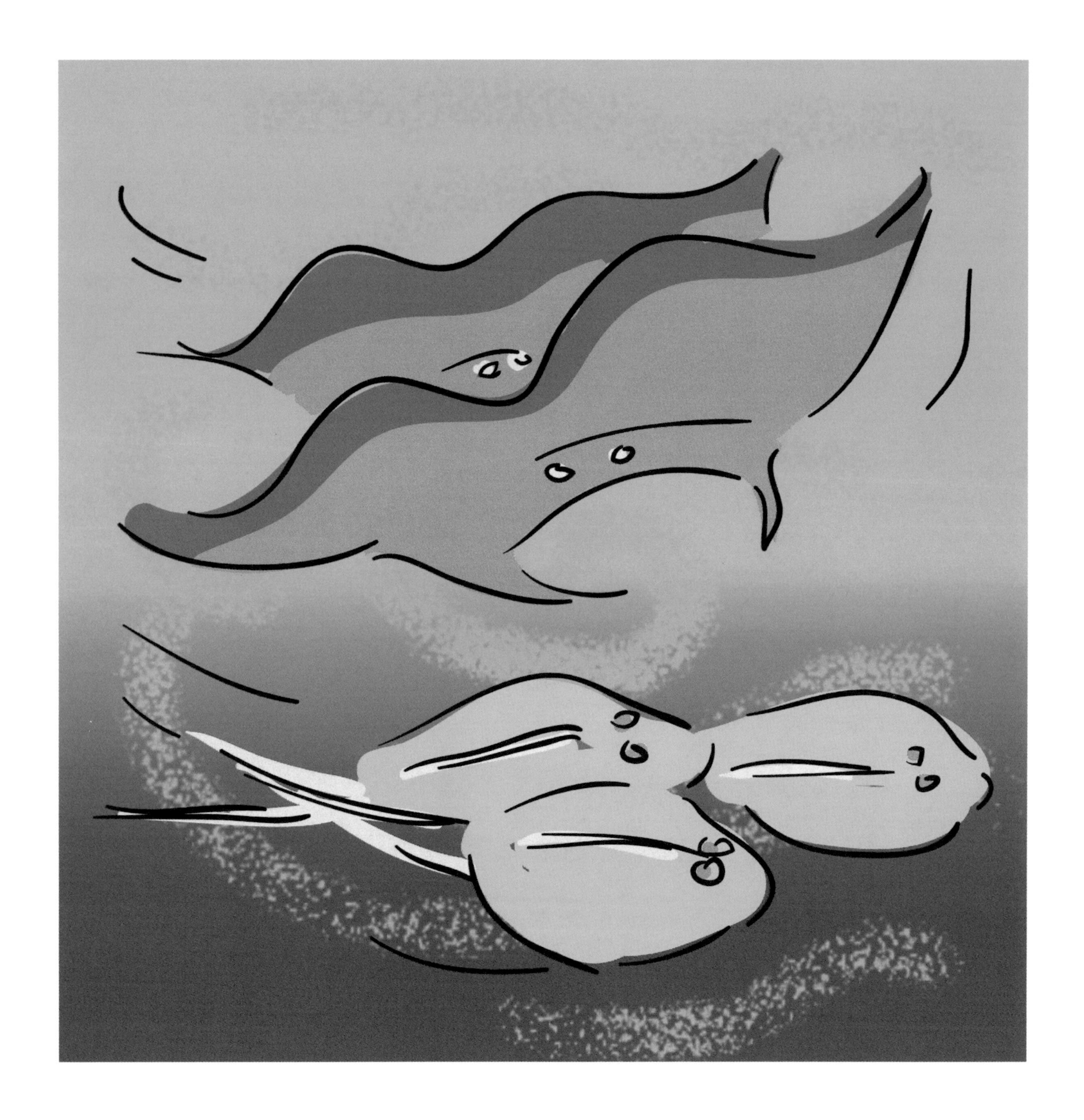

… and manta rays and stingrays.

It was all so exciting for Kevin. It was all so tiring for his turtle – for the turtle did the work. He carried the weight.

When they surfaced for the last time at the end of the day Kevin dropped his turtle on the shore as he had done before and rushed home in time for dinner. He left his poor, tired turtle to find food and drink for himself.

As the sun rose on the third day, Kevin arrived to find his turtle pulled into its shell.

Kevin knocked on the shell, “Come out! Come out! We have places to go.”

Slowly his turtle obeyed and struggled down to the water's edge. Kevin hopped on and pointed out to sea. "Let's go!" he yelled. He was filled with excitement for this new day's adventure.

“Out! Out!” he commanded. This time they swam so far out that they could barely see the shore when they looked back. But when they dove they could see what Kevin had wanted to see – dolphins and whales!

It was beyond his greatest dream. He petted the whales…

… and played tag with the dolphins. And, never during the day did he notice how tired his turtle was becoming. He was having too much fun himself to notice or care.

At the end of the day, Kevin waved goodbye to his friends and he and his turtle headed home. By the time they reached the shore it was very late and Kevin had no time to care for his turtle. He had to get home.

When he arrived the next morning bright and early, he had a hard time rousing his turtle. “Get up! Get up!” he shouted. There was no response. “I’ve got plans,” Kevin coaxed. His turtle did not move. It only opened its eyes a little, but still did not come out.

"A dunk in the water will wake you up," said Kevin, as he picked up his turtle and trudged to the shore. He dropped his turtle in the water, and then jumped on top.

His turtle sank!

"Now that's not the way a turtle is supposed to act," he said. He got off and tried again. "I've got plans," Kevin explained, but his turtle did not respond. He sank again.

"Never mind," said Kevin. He stomped out of the water and headed for the Turtle Keeper's shed. Knock! Knock! Knock!

The Turtle Keeper opened the door. “I need another turtle,” said Kevin.

“Sorry,” said the Turtle Keeper. “One turtle to a boy.”

“That’s it?” asked Kevin. “But I’ve got plans.”

“Well, you’re going to have to change your plans if they include a turtle.” Of course they included a turtle, he thought. It was the only way he could reach the magical world below. He had to be taken there on the back of a turtle. He suddenly realized, not just any turtle, but his turtle.

Kevin whirled around to see his turtle struggling to right himself in the water. It floundered on its back and seemed to be taking on water, sinking further with every wave.

“What’ll I do?” cried Kevin. He ran as fast as he could to the water’s edge. He threw himself into the water and swam to where he had last seen his turtle.

He reached down, grabbed the turtle's leg, pulled him up and tugged him to shore.

What'll I do now, wondered Kevin? He did the only thing he could think to do. He flipped and tipped his turtle in one direction and the other, draining all of the water out of him.

Then, he ran home and returned with a large bowl of chicken soup and very slowly fed it to his turtle.

Next, he built a shelter in some tall grass, away from the water and put his turtle in it for the night. The turtle was so grateful that he managed a little smile before Kevin left for home that evening.

The next day, Kevin raced to the shore, but this time his arms were full of gifts for his turtle. He had corn bread and peanut butter, radishes and lettuce. He had tomatoes, spinach and zucchini, and even an apple for dessert.

Little by little, day after day, as Kevin cared for his turtle, his turtle got better and stronger.

Eventually, he seemed well enough to go into the water again. Very gently Kevin led the turtle to the shore, then he put the turtle on his own back and swam out to sea.

There they dove and twirled, and as they both delighted in what they saw, Kevin thought to himself, I love the turtle on my back. And, it was clear that his turtle loved him.

From then on they took turns giving rides to each other and enjoying their adventures together. And from then on Kevin made sure that his turtle was fed well, got plenty of fresh air and lots and lots of rest.

The end,
but not the end
of caring for
each other.

At the end of this book you will find a Certificate of Merit that may be issued to any child who promises to honor the requirements stated in the Certificate. This fine Certificate will easily fit into a 5"x7" frame, and happily suit any girl or boy who receives it!

Here is another fun book by Sally Huss.

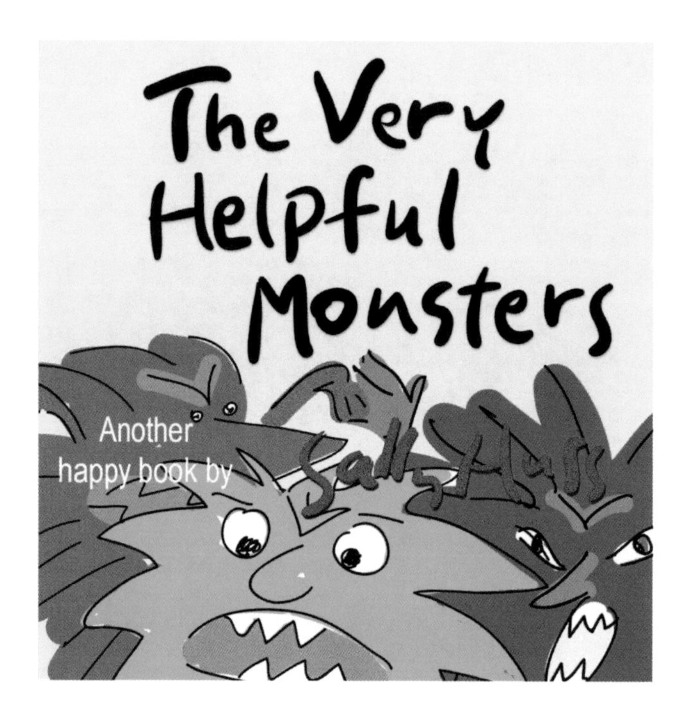

Description: Herbie was a very little fellow who knew exactly what he wanted to be – a monster. He had his reasons. Being small, he wanted others to notice him and he felt that there was no better way to do that than to become a monster.

So, he set out to find out how to become one. After finding no luck on his Internet searches for the information he needed, he decided he would get the real low-down on monsters from monsters themselves. One after another answered his questions and sent him off to interview another. But it was the fifth monster who put him straight. Changing his goals, Herbie decided that there was a better way to get what he wanted. What do you think he did?

Over 35 amusing and colorful illustrations accompany this charming story.

To learn more about THE VERY HELPFUL MONSTERS go to http://amzn.com/B00IDSNR7E.

If you liked KEVIN AND HIS MAGIC TURTLE, please be kind enough to post a short review on Amazon. Here is the link: http://amzn.com/B00LUAM1F6.

You may wish to join our Family of Friends to receive information about upcoming FREE e-book promotions and download a free poster – "Happiness on an Elephant" on Sally's website -- http://www.sallyhuss.com. Thank You.

More Sally Huss books may be viewed on the Author's Profile on Amazon. Here is that URL: http://amzn.to/VpR7B8.

About the Author/Illustrator

Sally Huss

"Bright and happy," "light and whimsical" have been the catch phrases attached to the writings and art of Sally Huss for over 30 years. Sweet images dance across all of Sally's creations, whether in the form of children's books, paintings, wallpaper, ceramics, baby bibs, purses, clothing, or her King Features syndicated newspaper panel "Happy Musings."

Sally creates children's books to uplift the lives of children and hopes you will join her in this effort by helping spread her happy messages.

Sally is a graduate of USC with a degree in Fine Art and through the years has had 26 of her own licensed art galleries throughout the world.

This certificate may be cut out, framed, and presented to any child who has demonstrated her or his worthiness to receive it.

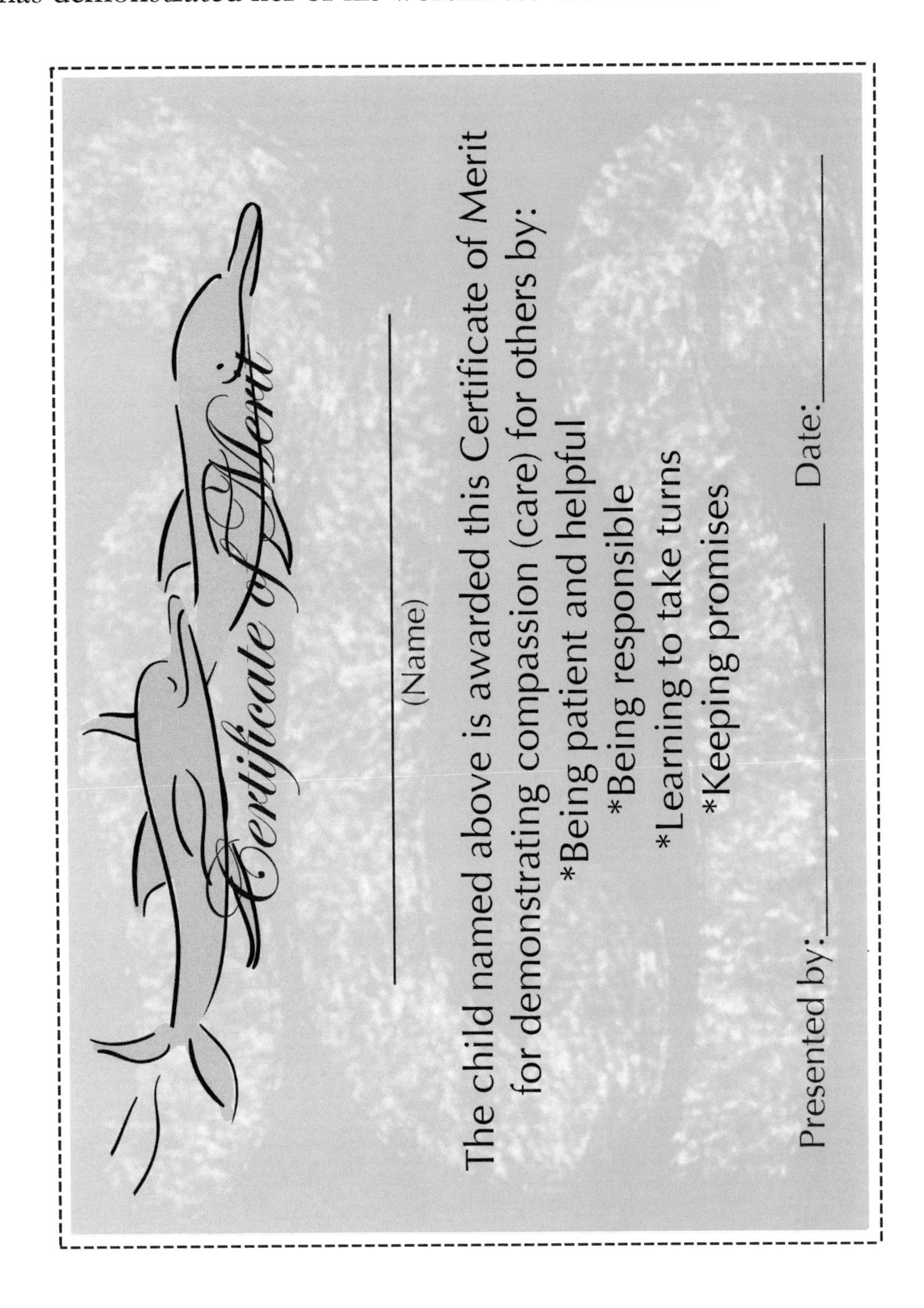

Made in the USA
Lexington, KY
03 May 2016